A ROOKIE READER®

BOBBY'S ZOO

By Carolyn Lunn

Illustrations by Tom Dunnington

Prepared under the direction of Robert Hillerich, Ph.D.

CHILDRENS PRESS®

CHICAGO

LIBRARY OF CONGRESS
Library of Congress Cataloging-in-Publication Data

Lunn, Carolyn.
    Bobby's zoo / by Carolyn Lunn ; Tom Dunnington,
illustrator.
        p.   cm. — (A Rookie reader)
    Summary: Bobby doesn't know what to do with all
the animals that are in his house.
    ISBN 0-516-02089-7
    [1. Animals—Fiction. 2. Humorous stories.]
I. Dunnington, Tom, ill. II. Title. III. Series.
PZ7.L979118Bo   1989
[E]—dc19   88-36865
                                                CIP
                                                 AC

    9 10 11 12 13 14 15 16 R 02 01

My house is full of animals.
Tell me what to do.

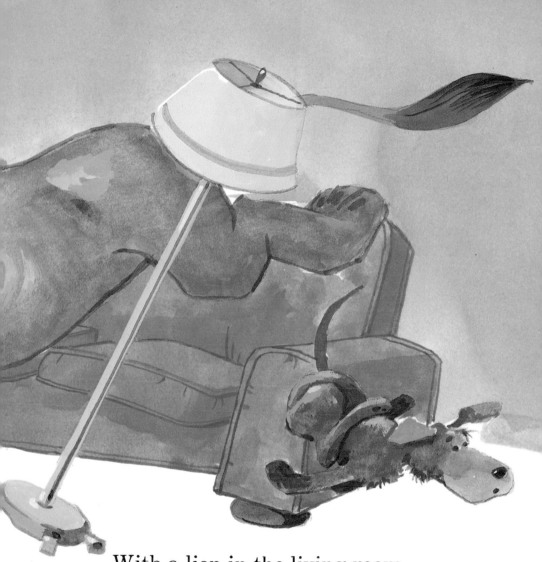

With a lion in the living room,

a kitchen kangaroo,

8

an elephant in the garden,

a seal in the bath,

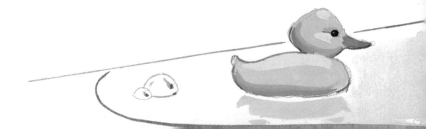

a hippo in the hall,

and a singing giraffe.

14

15

A camel in the closet,

a snake on the stairs,

a penguin eating ice cream,

a bedroom full of bears,

a parrot in the pantry,

a zebra making bread,

a tiger on the telephone,
and a monkey on his head.

My house is full of animals,

tell me what to do.

30

Open it on Saturday
and call it Bobby's zoo?

WORD LIST

a	elephant	kitchen	Saturday
an	full	lion	seal
and	garden	living	singing
animals	giraffe	making	snake
bath	hall	me	stairs
bears	head	monkey	telephone
bedroom	hippo	my	tell
Bobby's	his	of	the
bread	house	on	tiger
call	ice cream	open	to
camel	in	pantry	what
closet	is	parrot	with
do	it	penguin	zebra
eating	kangaroo	room	zoo

About the Author

Carolyn Lunn is an American, now living in England with her British husband and three-year-old son. As well as writing stories, she enjoys running, cooking, and gardening. Her other books include *A Whisper Is Quiet* and *Purple Is Part of a Rainbow*.

About the Artist

Tom Dunnington divides his time between book illustration and wildlife painting. He has done many books for Childrens Press, as well as working on textbooks, and is a regular contributor to "Highlights for Children." Tom lives in Oak Park, Illinois.